SANTA MAKES A CHANGE

written by SOL CHANELES
illustrated by JEROME SNYDER

Parents' Magazine Press • New York

Text Copyright © 1970 by Sol Chaneles. Illustrations Copyright © 1970 by Jerome Snyder. All rights reserved. Printed in the United States of America. ISBN: Trade 0-8193-0428-X, Library 0-8193-0429-8. Library of Congress Catalog Card Number: 74-117557.

SANTA sat in his easy chair. He was darning the sleeve of his jacket.

Goodness, he thought, it's been a long time since I had a new suit. I wonder . . .

Santa walked to the window and watched the polar bears dancing on the lawn. He thought and thought and thought.

"An important decision like this calls for everyone's opinion," he said.

Santa went to the telephone. He pushed the button marked HELPERS.

"I would like," Santa announced, "all my helpers to attend a special meeting at once."

Then Santa pushed a button marked REINDEER.

"I would like all my reindeer to come to a special meeting at once."

Then Santa made a call to Jack Frost, inviting him to come, too.

In a moment they were all gathered in his large, warm office.

"I called this meeting," Santa said, "because I think it is time for me to make a change."

"A change!" exclaimed his seventy-three helpers.

"A change?" asked the reindeer, stamping their hooves restlessly.

"You heard him," said Jack Frost, who was sometimes a bit sharp. And then a drop of water rolled off his nose as he melted for just a moment. "Santa is entitled to a change after so many years," said Jack.

"I hope you don't mean us," everyone murmured as they looked anxiously to the left and right. "We like it here," they said.

"Oh, no," said Santa. "You are my dear fellow workers and friends!"

"Well then? Well then?" said Jack Frost.

"I mean this old suit of mine," said Santa. "Nobody wears knickers and black boots anymore. Why, do you know that last Christmas one little boy thought my red hat was a nightcap!

"And this jacket," said Santa. "Nobody wears loose, floppy jackets anymore. No, I *must* make a change of costume."

Everyone was very embarrassed.

Sebastian, a foreman in the toy fire engine department at Santa's workshop, looked out of the corner of his eye at the other helpers. Santa had given every one of them a new suit last Christmas.

Jack Frost had just had his fur coat glazed and restyled. Even the reindeer shed every year and sported brand new coats and bright shiny antlers.

No one had given a thought to Santa's old, worn baggy red suit. They had just taken him for granted.

"Well," said Dasher, the reindeer, "speaking on behalf of the shipping department, I certainly am in favor of anything that makes you feel good."

Santa thanked him.

"And the helpers," said Sebastian, "Picolo, Tiny Tom and all the rest of us, are one hundred percent behind you."

Santa smiled. "And you, Jack Frost?"

"Clear as an ice crystal," said Jack Frost. "Whatever Santa wants to do is supercilious with me."

Jack sometimes liked to use big words and didn't always know what they meant. His friends tried not to notice.

"What kind of outfit did you have in mind?" asked Sebastian.

"I don't know," Santa said. "Why don't we go into the clothing department, and I'll try on a few things and see how they look."

"Something dashing," said Dancer.

"Something dancing," said Dasher. They giggled. Sometimes they acted like very silly reindeer.

In the clothing department there were great racks of new outfits. Santa looked at the assortment.

"A uniform," said Picolo, "one like the brass band wears when they change the guard at Buckingham Palace."

"Oh, wonderful," everyone said.

Santa disappeared for a moment. He returned in a glorious, bright new uniform of the Coldstream Guards.

"Very handsome," everyone said. And Santa preened himself.

"Of course," said Jack Frost, "that tight jacket is not too becoming to your rather—er—mature figure."

He means, thought Santa, that I look fat.

"That big fur hat," said Donner, who was a practical reindeer. "Won't that blow off in a strong wind?"

"And the sword," said Elmer, another helper. "It might get hung up in a chimney."

"Hmm," said Santa Claus. "It would be a lot of work keeping these brass buttons polished. Shall I try something else?"

"Yes!" they all shouted.

"How about a Scottish bagpiper's outfit?" said Angus, a helper from Glasgow. "Och mon, I dearly love a bonny piper."

"Wonderful," everyone said politely, though they really thought it was a silly idea.

Santa appeared in a moment wearing a gay bonnet with a feather, a short tweed jacket, a plaid kilt, knee-length plaid stockings, and gaiters, which are little affairs that strap under the shoes and hug the ankles.

He blew a note on the bagpipes, and everyone held their ears except Angus, who spun and jumped happily in a Scottish dance.

"I'll try very hard not to nip your knees, Santa," said Jack Frost. "You're going to be very uncomfortable if you're out when I have to deliver a blizzard or a north wind."

"Oh dear," said Cupid, a pretty reindeer with a sweet voice. "Oh dear, we can't have Santa catching cold."

"That feather will blow right off," warned Vixen. "And I really don't think those stockings are too flattering to your legs."

Santa looked down at his chubby knees. They felt cold already.

He sneezed. *Achoo!* "Well, I do look handsome. But I don't think this is a practical costume for someone who goes flying in outer space."

"That's it!" said Dudley, a helper who worked on scientific toys. "What you need is a spaceman's outfit."

"How modern," everyone said.

"How practical."

"How up to date."

"How tight," Santa said in a muffled voice. He had slipped on a rubber space suit and a plastic helmet. He said something else but no one could hear him. And there was a terrible moment of confusion as they tried to unscrew the helmet.

"That was awful," Santa said. "Simply awful. I felt like a jar of peach preserves."

"You've got to get used to it," said Dudley.
"Can't," said Santa. "It squeezes my chest."
Everyone knew that Santa meant his stomach.

"I have it," said Shanthu, who helped Santa make jewelry for people in India. "A most elegant and impressive costume is that of an Indian policeman."

"Don't like it," said Dudley.

"Inappropriate," said Angus.

"He could try it on," said Cupid, who was very fond of Shanthu.

In a twinkling, Santa stood before them and how grand and stern he looked. A gorgeous turban was wound around his head. A fresh white uniform sat grandly on his sturdy shoulders. Knee-length shorts

and knee stockings completed the outfit. Across his chest blazed a cluster of medals.

"I'll nae have it," said Angus. "If he can't wear kilts, he can't wear shorts."

"Well," said Santa, who didn't want to offend anyone, "it's very pretty. But perhaps the material is a bit light for winter wear."

He then tried on a Davy Crockett outfit . . .

a railway engineer's cap and overalls...

the uniform of a Swiss guard...

a cowboy suit with a ten-gallon hat.

He appeared as a knight in shining armor,

a Chinese mandarin,

an Indian chief.

He slipped on a barge captain's uniform

and even a cook's outfit, which everyone agreed was
inappropriate.

"Dear me," Santa said. "This is so difficult."

"Dear me," said Dasher, Dancer, Prancer, Vixen, Comet and—you know—all the rest.

"Old, familiar things are so hard to replace when you love them," said Santa.

"Just like Santa," said Jack Frost, who looked as though he was about to melt again.

Everyone fell silent for a moment.

"Dear Santa," said Cupid, "could we see you again, just once, in that nice red suit with that white fur trim?"

"Yes," said Picolo. "And those fine shiny black boots?"

"Don't make boots like that anymore," Sebastian said with a sigh.

Everyone looked at Santa Claus when he stood in front of them, pulling the soft black belt around his red velvet jacket.

There was a moment of silence and then a burst of applause.

The polar bears stopped playing and ran to the window.

"Wonderful," everyone said.

"How smart."

"How handsome."

"How really like Christmas," said Dudley.

"Well," Santa said, "perhaps I'll keep this outfit a little longer. There is still a lot of wear left in it. And besides, how would all the little boys and girls know me without it? I think," said Santa, "I'll write a poem."

And this is the poem that Santa wrote:

My suit is not the latest thing.
It's somewhat worn in places,
But people know me when I bring
A smile to children's faces.